Wombat
DIVINE

★

written by Mem Fox

illustrated by
Kerry Argent

Omnibus Books

To Sue and Jane, Publishers Divine
– M.F.

For Michael

For Patricia and Stephen

Heartfelt thanks for your support.
– K.A.

Promotion of this title has been assisted by
the South Australian Government through the
Department for the Arts and Cultural Development.

Kerry Argent used watercolour and coloured pencils
for the illustrations in this book.

Omnibus Books
A.C.N. 000 614 577
52 Fullarton Road, Norwood, South Australia 5067
part of the SCHOLASTIC AUSTRALIA GROUP
Sydney · Auckland · New York · Toronto · London

First published 1995
First published in this edition 1995

Text copyright © Mem Fox 1995
Illustrations copyright © Kerry Argent 1995

Typeset by Clinton Ellicott, Adelaide
Produced in Australia by Griffin Colour.

National Library of Australia Cataloguing-in-Publication entry
Fox, Mem, 1946–   .
Wombat divine.
ISBN 1 86291 283 1.
1. Wombats – Juvenile fiction. I. Argent, Kerry, 1960–   .
II. Title.

A823.3

It was the week before Christmas.
Wombat loved Christmas.
He loved the carols and the candles,
the presents and the pudding,
but most of all he loved the Nativity Play.

For as long as he could remember
Wombat had wanted to be in the Nativity.
Now, at last, he was old enough to take part.
So, with his heart full of hope
and his head full of dreams,
he hurried along to the auditions.

His friends were already there.

Emu was bossing and fussing as usual.
"Now, let's get started," she said.
"Who'd like to be the Archangel Gabriel?"

"I would," said Wombat.

But he was too heavy to be the Archangel Gabriel.

Bilby was chosen instead.

Bilby patted Wombat on the back.
"Never mind, Wombat! Don't lose heart.
Why not try for a different part?"

"What a good idea," said Emu. "Now who'd like to be Mary?"

"I would," said Wombat.

But he was too big to be Mary.

Numbat was chosen instead.

Numbat stroked Wombat's nose.
"There, there, Wombat! Don't lose heart.
Why not try for a different part?"

"Right," said Emu. "Now who'd like to be
one of the Three Kings?"

"I would," said Wombat.

But he was too short to be a king.

The Kangaroos were chosen instead.

The Kangaroos put their arms around Wombat.
"Cheer up, Wombat! Don't lose heart.
Why not try for a different part?"

Wombat tried everything.

He wanted to be Joseph,

but he was too sleepy.

He wanted to be the innkeeper,
but he was too clumsy.

He wanted to be one of the shepherds,

but he was too short-sighted.

And then there were no parts left.

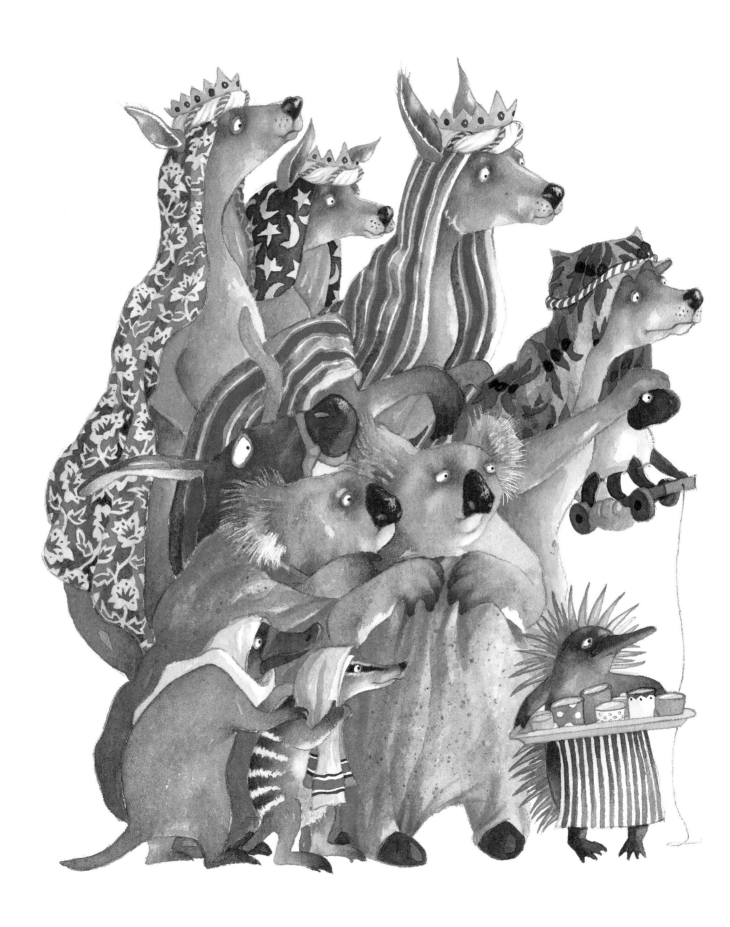

Wombat hung his head
and hoped he wouldn't cry.

Suddenly Bilby leapt into the air.
"I know!" he shouted.
"You could be the Baby Jesus!"

"Could I?" asked Wombat.
"Could I really?"

"Of course you could, Wombat," said Emu.
"Fancy my forgetting such an important part!
A Nativity without the Baby Jesus
is no Nativity at all."

Wombat was dizzy with pride.

Christmas Eve arrived at last.
Everyone was nervous except Wombat.
He lay quiet and still
throughout the whole performance.

He even fell asleep,
just as a real baby would.

On Christmas Day, when everyone was
opening presents and eating pudding,
they all agreed it had been the best Nativity ever.

"You were divine, Wombat!" said Emu.

And Wombat beamed.